Bobbie Dazzler

Written by
Margaret Wild

Illustrated by
Janine Dawson

Kane/Miller
BOOK PUBLISHERS

For Olivia,
who loves to jump and hop and skip – M.W.

For my mum and dad – J.D.

Janine Dawson used pen and ink and watercolor
for the illustrations in this book.

Kane/Miller Book Publishers, Inc.
First American Edition 2007
by Kane/Miller Book Publishers, Inc.
La Jolla, California

Originally published in Australia in 2006 by Working Title Press, Kingswood, SA

Text copyright © Margaret Wild 2006
Illustrations copyright © Janine Dawson 2006

All rights reserved. For information contact:
Kane/Miller Book Publishers, Inc.
P.O. Box 8515
La Jolla, CA 92038
www.kanemiller.com

Library of Congress Control Number: 2007921049
Printed and bound in China
2 3 4 5 6 7 8 9 10

ISBN: 978-1-933605-46-3

The character of Bobbie is based on the Red-necked Wallaby (*Macropus rufogriseus*),
which is found in the coastal forests of eastern Australia and so named because of the
rust-red fur across its shoulders and the back of its neck.

Bobbie could jump.

And bounce.

And skip.

She could hop on her left leg.

And on her right leg.

But she could not do the splits!

"Never mind," said Koala.

But Bobbie minded.
A lot.

Bobbie could walk on her heels.

She could walk on her toes.

She could balance on a fallen log.

She could whirl ...

... and twirl.

But she could not do the splits!

"Never mind," said Wombat.

But Bobbie minded. A lot.

She could stand on her head.

She could do hand springs.

She could do somersaults –

forwards …

... and backwards.

But she could *not* do the splits!

"Never mind," said Possum.

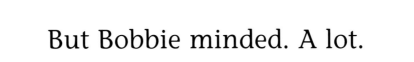

But Bobbie minded. A lot.

One morning, Bobbie said, "This time I will do it.
I will! I will! I will!"

She closed her eyes. She took a deep breath.

Then she slid ... and slid ... and sliiiiiidd.

"Look!" she said. "I've done the splits!"

"Dazzling, Bobbie! Dazzling!" everyone said.

But Bobbie couldn't get up. She was stuck.

"Oh dear," said Koala, Wombat and Possum.

But Bobbie didn't mind. Not at all.

Because now that she'd done the splits once,
she knew she could do them again perfectly.

And, after lots

and lots

and *lots* of practice,

so could Koala, Wombat and Possum!